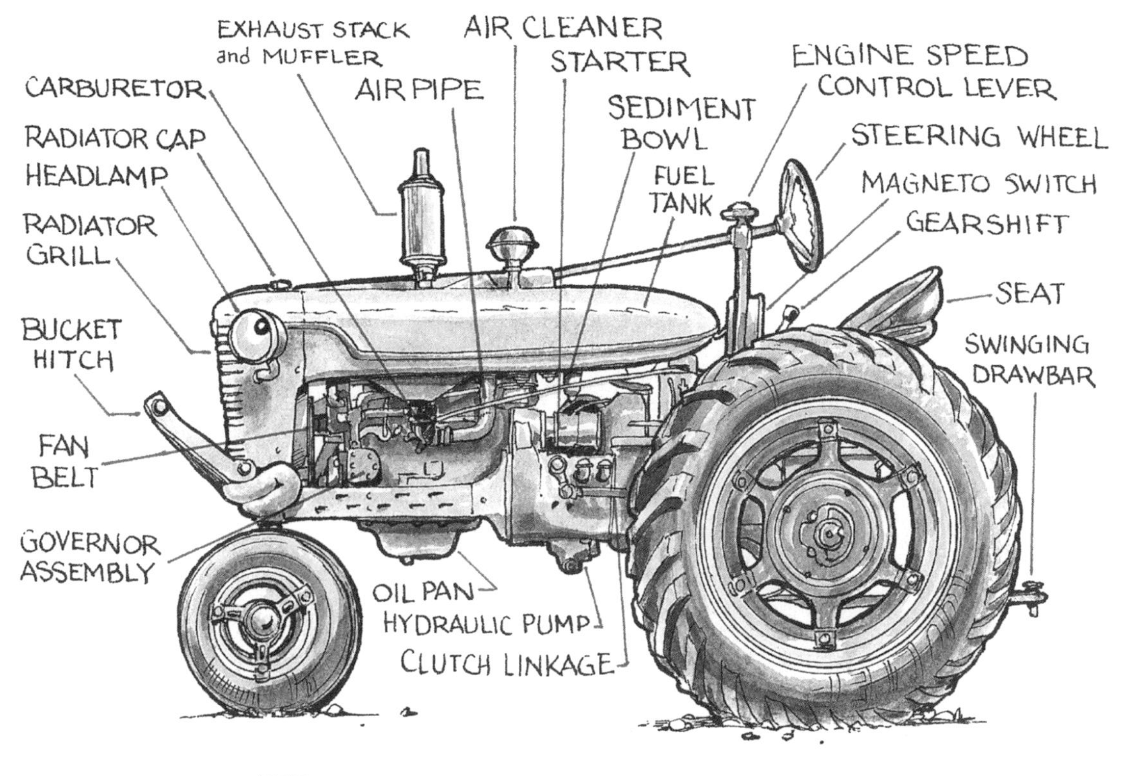
EXHAUST STACK and MUFFLER
AIR CLEANER
STARTER
ENGINE SPEED CONTROL LEVER
CARBURETOR
AIR PIPE
SEDIMENT BOWL
STEERING WHEEL
RADIATOR CAP
HEADLAMP
FUEL TANK
MAGNETO SWITCH
RADIATOR GRILL
GEARSHIFT
SEAT
BUCKET HITCH
SWINGING DRAWBAR
FAN BELT
GOVERNOR ASSEMBLY
OIL PAN
HYDRAULIC PUMP
CLUTCH LINKAGE

Tractor Mac

To Jinx and Stu,
and the whole Lewis clan.
Parades are best viewed
from your store window.

Tractor Mac, Inc., Roxbury, CT 06783 USA
Visit www.tractormac.com

Tractor Mac
PARADE'S BEST

written and illustrated by Billy Steers

Tractor Mac and Sam the Ram watched as the floats and decorations were made ready for the big town parade.

"I've never seen so many fabulous floats," said Sam. "What a parade this will be! Which float will you pull, Tractor Mac?"

"I don't know," answered Tractor Mac. "I just know Mrs. J. is driving. I hope I get to pull the parade's best float!"

"Maybe you'll pull the Young Farmers Float." said Carla the Chicken. "I'd like that," said Tractor Mac.

"You can't pull that float," whinnied Sibley the workhorse. "The Young Farmers Club will ride on my wagon in the parade.

Maybe you could pull the float for the Outdoor Club."

“Already taken,” said a familiar voice. “They asked me to pull the Outdoor Club’s float this year,” said Mac’s friend, Wink.

"What about the Kid's Club float or the Sport Team float?" asked Wink.

FUN
JOIN
PLAY & LEARN
KID'S CLUB

"You can't pull those floats," said Lucy. "Small Fred and I are pulling those floats." "GO-TEAM-GO!" cheered Small Fred. "Which float will be left for me to pull?" wondered Tractor Mac. "So many good floats have been taken already."

“Well, you can’t pull this one,” grunted a deep voice. It was Deke. “I always pull the big Fair Float. I win the tractor pulling contests at the fair, you know.”

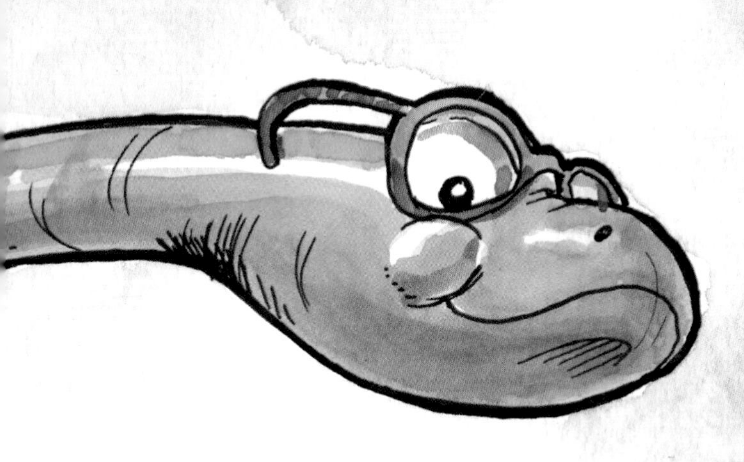

"I remember," said Mac. "You're hard to beat."

"Very tough," agreed Sam the ram.

"Tucker Pick-up is pulling the Fishing Club float," said Paul the pig. "You can't pull that float."

"Carl's pulling the patriotic float," said Pete the pig. "You can't pull that float."

"Wait Tractor Mac," said Margot the cow. "There's one float left. That float must be the one Mrs. J wants you to pull." "Oh! No-No-NO!" cried Tractor Mac. "I CAN'T pull THAT float in the parade!"

Petals
Posies
Ribbons

It was the Petals and Posies, Ribbons and Roses float. "You'll be the cutest tractor in the parade," laughed Sam the ram. "It smells good enough to eat!" mooed Margot.

"Now I need to decorate Tractor Mac," said Mrs. J. "We don't have much time." But Tractor Mac was gone.

The open garage was a good place to hide.
“They won’t find me in here,” thought Mac.
“Posies and rosies! I can’t pull that float.
Everybody will laugh at me!”

Tractor Mac had never been in the garage before. It was filled with boxes, tools and old photos on the wall. One photo reminded Tractor Mac of Mrs. J.

"That was me as a little girl," said Mrs. J walking in. "My, that was a long time ago. I loved that toy pedal tractor, but now I have you, Tractor Mac. Do you think we could be 'Parade's Best' together?"

Tractor Mac looked at the picture again. "Of course I can pull that float," smiled Mac. "We can be Parade's Best!"

“We’ve got to hurry or we’ll miss
the parade!” said the ladies in
their big flowery hats.

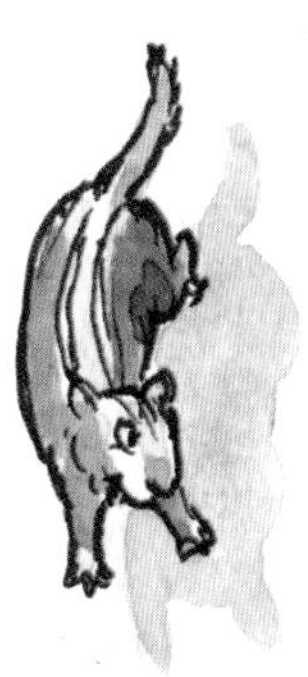

“Hurry! Hurry! Hurry!”

Flowers flew, bows bounced. The ladies of the Petals and Posies, Ribbons and Roses Club held on tightly.

Tractor Mac and Mrs. J. raced to town.
"You can still make it," cheered Sam the Ram.

Cheers and applause greeted the big flowery float pulled by

Bands played. Teams marched. Balloons and flags bobbed and

There were clowns and jugglers, dancers and bagpipers,

the bright red tractor at the end of the parade.

waved. There were firemen, policemen, soldiers and sailors.

trucks, tractors and motorcycles.

"Glad you made it," chuckled Sibley. "Mrs. J sure looks proud." Tractor Mac laughed. "I couldn't miss my chance to pull the Parade's Best!"

Billy Steers is an author, illustrator, and pilot. In addition to the Tractor Mac series, he has worked on forty other children's books. Mr. Steers had horses and sheep on the farm where he grew up in Roxbury, Connecticut. Married with three sons, he still lives in Roxbury.

Tractor Mac™

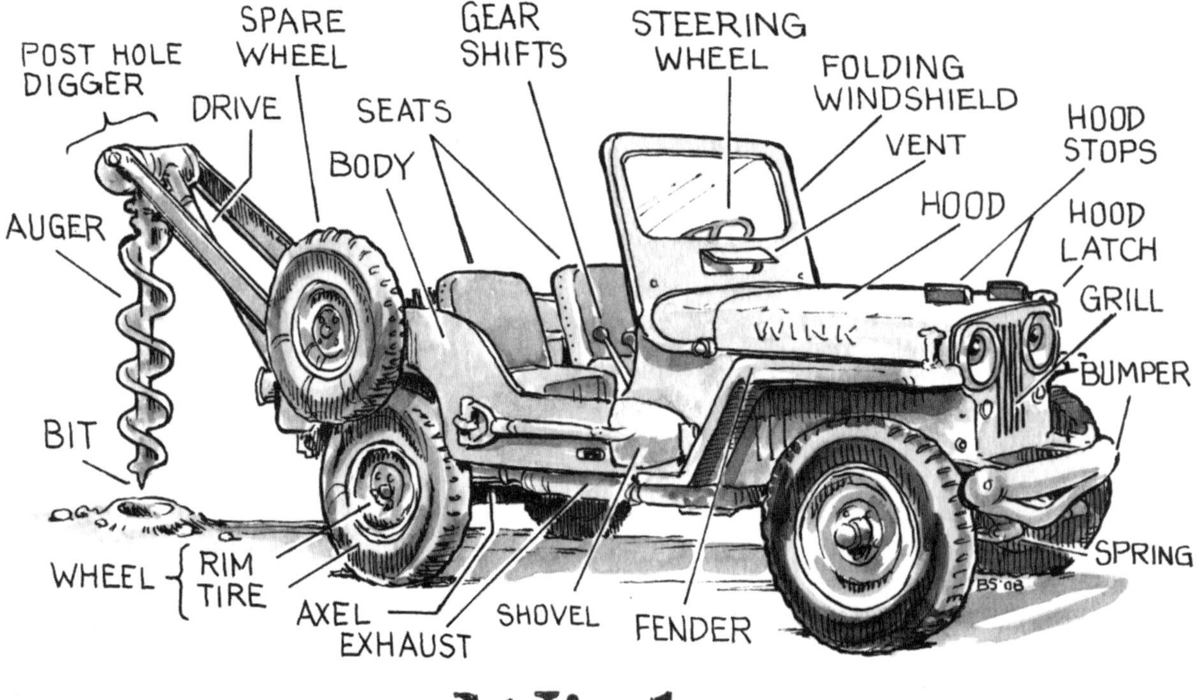
POST HOLE DIGGER
SPARE WHEEL
GEAR SHIFTS
STEERING WHEEL
FOLDING WINDSHIELD
DRIVE
SEATS
VENT
HOOD STOPS
BODY
HOOD
AUGER
HOOD LATCH
GRILL
WINK
BUMPER
BIT
SPRING
WHEEL
RIM
TIRE
AXEL
EXHAUST
SHOVEL
FENDER
BS'08

Wink